A TEMPLAR BOOK

This book is based on the television series *Gigantosaurus*™.
The TV series *Gigantosaurus*™ is created and produced by Cyber Group Studios.
Based on the original characters created by Jonny Duddle in the book *Gigantosaurus*,
first published by Templar Books in 2014.

First published in the UK in 2020 by Templar Books,
an imprint of Bonnier Books UK,
The Plaza, 535 King's Road, London, SW10 0SZ
Owned by Bonnier Books, Sveavägen 56, Stockholm, Sweden
www.templarco.co.uk
www.bonnierbooks.co.uk

5 7 9 10 8 6

ISBN 978-1-78741-569-0

Written and edited by Phoebe Jascourt and Carly Blake
Designed by Dynamo Limited
Additional design by Adam Allori
Production Controller Ché Creasey

Printed in Latvia

THE STORY OF GIGANTOSAURUS™

templar
books

Meet the DINOS . . .

MAZU

BILL

TINY

ROCKY

GIGANTOSAURUS

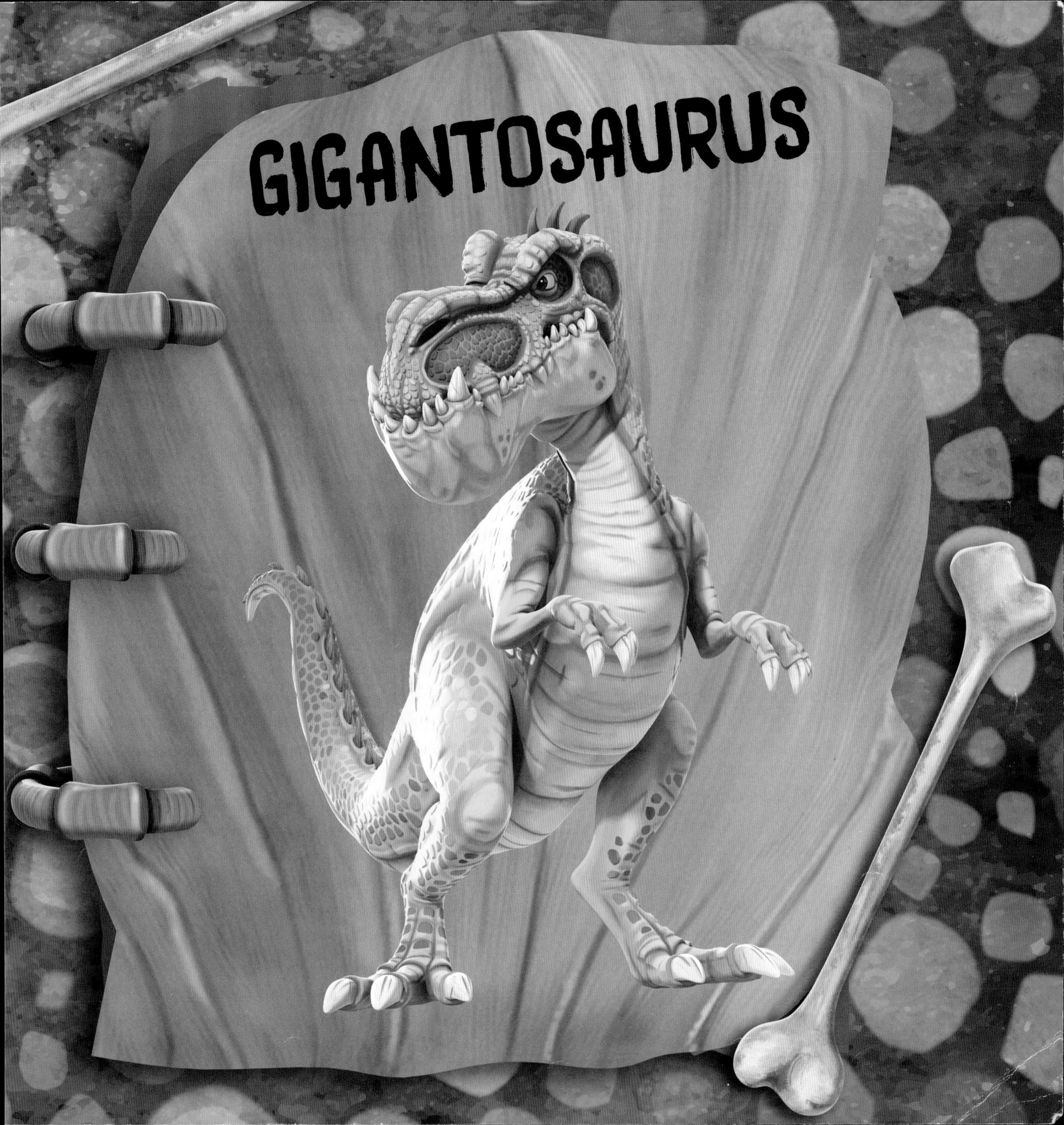

Once upon a time in the Cretaceous world, millions of years ago, dinosaurs roamed the earth. They were the most massive creatures that ever existed. With their pointy claws, sharp teeth and fearsome roars, these creatures were TERRIFYING . . .

. . . well, most of them.

I must write that down in my Gigantopedia!

I'm a para... a parasolo... a parasoph... a dinosaur!

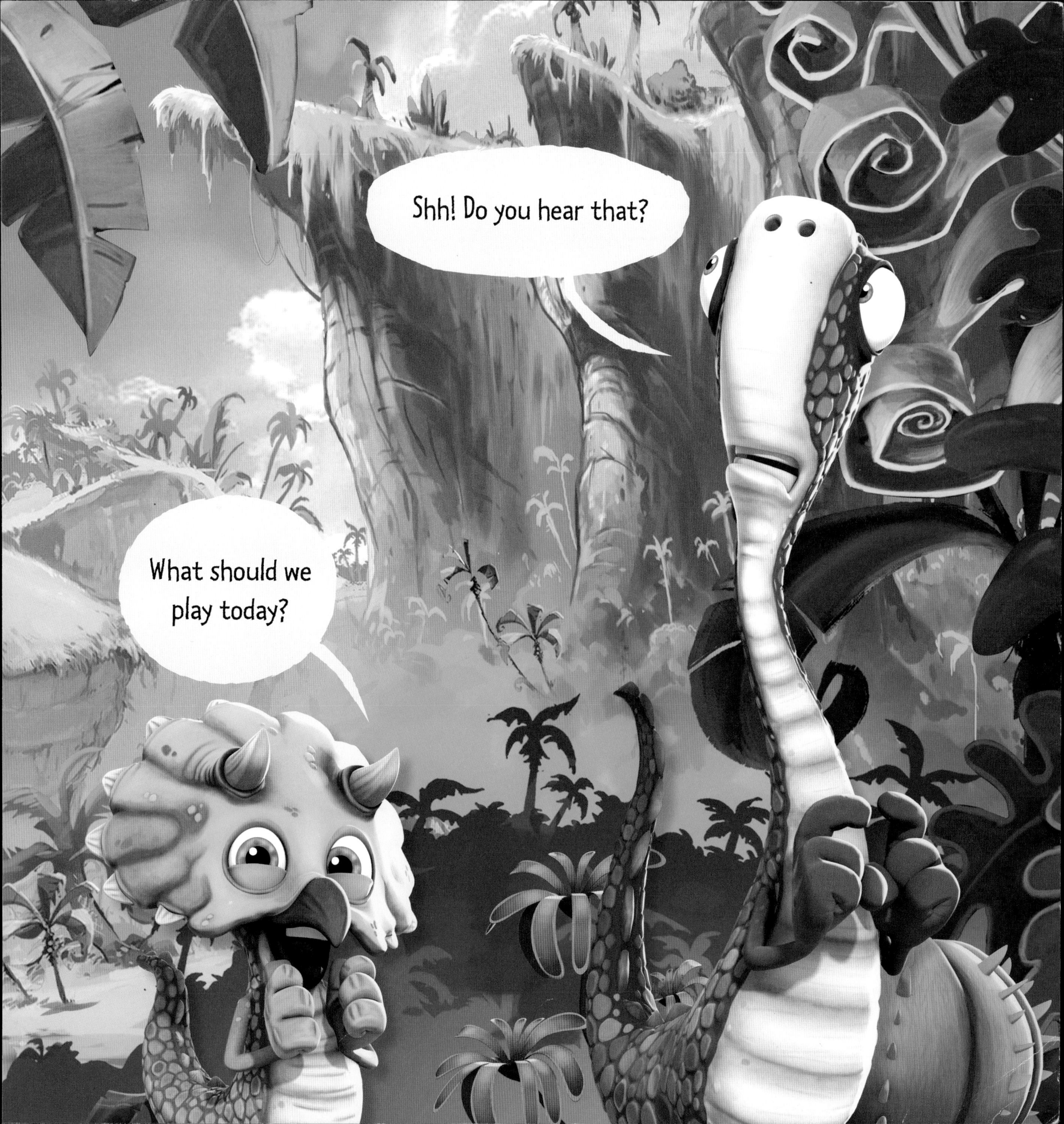
Shh! Do you hear that?
What should we play today?

Mazu was a curious young ankylosaurus who loved to learn new things. Whenever she discovered a new fact she'd write it in her trusty Gigantopedia.

Want to hang out?

Rocky, the little parasaurolophus, was always looking for new adventures. He certainly wasn't afraid of a little danger – he'd usually run towards it!

I may be small, but I'm TOUGH!

Unlike Rocky, Bill was a nervous dinosaur.
Even though he'd one day grow into
a HUGE brachiosaurus, he was
nowhere near as fearless
as his friends.

Where am I?

These flowers
are so pretty!

Tiny was a triceratops who loved
having fun. She could usually be found
drawing, singing and making friends.

Although the four friends were very different,
they always had a great time together. They made musical
instruments with bamboo sticks, went swinging on jungle
vines and snacked on tasty coconuts all day.

All in all, they had a pretty great life. There was just one thing that could ruin their day . . .

. . . GIGANTOSAURUS!

He was the largest, most dangerous dinosaur in the whole of the Cretaceous world, and he was ALWAYS hungry.

The dinos were terrified of Gigantosaurus, but they were also fascinated by him. What was his favourite thing to do? Where did he hang out? What did he like to eat? (Hopefully not baby dinos!)

All they knew for sure was that at the sound of Giganto's stomps, you had to . . .

RUN!

One day, Mazu had an idea.

"Let's go Gigantosaurus hunting," she suggested.

"We can finally find out where he hides away all day!"

Tiny and Rocky were very excited. Bill, on the other hand, wasn't so sure.

No way! He's just too scary!

But Mazu was determined. She armed her friends with some handy tools for their adventure – a leafy spyglass, a sundial and some coconuts (Giganto hunting was thirsty work!). In no time at all they were ready to go.

They headed to the deepest part of the jungle –
the perfect hiding place for a **MASSIVE** dinosaur.

"This would be a great spot for Giganto to
get some peace and quiet," said Mazu
thoughtfully.

"Then is it really the best idea
to disturb him?" Bill replied,
trembling with fear.

Let's just
go home!

"Hey, look up there!" Tiny said excitedly, pointing at a shape high up in the trees. They crept forward to get a closer look.

"Oh no," Mazu sighed. "It's only Archie the archaeopteryx."

What do you mean 'ONLY'?

Determined, Mazu led her friends out of the jungle and into
the savannah. The volcano up ahead with its fiery lava seemed like
an ideal spot for a TERRIFYING dinosaur to spend his days.

"I bet Giganto thinks we'd be way too scared to disturb
him here!" Mazu said.

The young dinosaurs eagerly followed. Even Bill was starting
to feel excited that they may finally find Gigantosaurus's hangout

The friends spotted a figure in the distance and slowly made their way closer. But this time, they ran into Dilo the dilophosaurus.

Sorry! No Giganto here.

Bill, Rocky and Tiny were tired and hungry, and were starting to think they'd never find Gigantosaurus.

"You can't give up now!" Mazu cried. So the dinosaurs trudged on to the lake.

We are not quitters!

At the lake, all was calm.
Until suddenly, the ENORMOUS
Terminonator lunged out of
the water towards the little
dinos! She opened her
mouth and revealed
her huge spiky teeth.

ARGHHH!

Mazu, Tiny, Rocky and Bill charged away
as fast as they could. Up ahead, they saw a
dark cave, so Mazu grabbed her friends and
darted towards it. They all fell inside
and tried to catch their breath.

I guess we'll never
find Giganto . . .

At least we're
safe now!

These rocks look VERY jagged!

They got up and started to explore the cave. They'd never been to this place before! It was warm, damp and a little bit smelly . . .

Errr, g-g-guys . . .

Suddenly, a deafening ROAR erupted around them. The dinosaurs jumped up in fear.

"I don't think this is a cave . . ." began Mazu nervously. "I think we're inside GIGANTO'S MOUTH!"

ARGHHH!

The dinosaurs ran and ran until they were safely back in the jungle.
"We ran away too quickly to see where he lives, but I did learn something new about Giganto . . ." Mazu said happily as she wrote in her Gigantopedia.

He has REALLY smelly breath.